Special thanks to Linda Chapman
To Clara Westwood – may all your
wishes come true!

ORCHARD BOOKS

First published in Great Britain in 2016 by The Watts Publishing Group

1 3 5 7 9 10 8 6 4 2

Text copyright © Hothouse Fiction, 2016
Illustrations copyright © Orchard Books, 2016

A CIP catalogue record for this book
is available from the British Library.

ISBN 978 1 40833 614 4

Printed and bound in Great Britain by Clays Ltd, St Ives plc

The paper and board used in this book are made from wood from responsible sources.

Orchard Books
An imprint of
Hachette Children's Group
Part of The Watts Publishing Group Limited
Carmelite House
50 Victoria Embankment
London EC4Y 0DZ

An Hachette UK Company
www.hachette.co.uk
www.hachettechildrens.co.uk

Series created by Hothouse Fiction
www.hothousefiction.com

Pop Princess

ROSIE BANKS

Wishing Star Palace

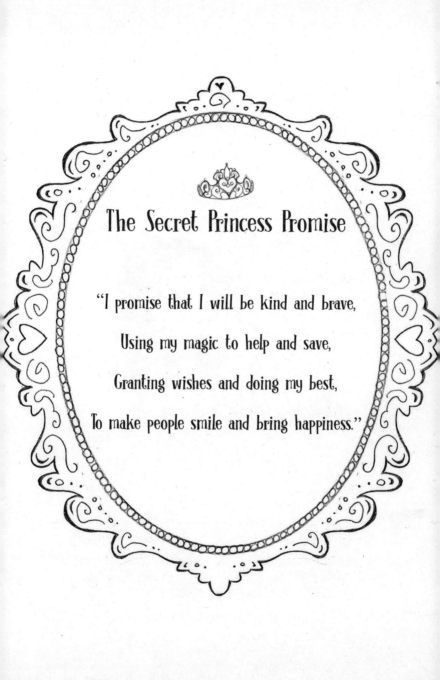

The Secret Princess Promise

"I promise that I will be kind and brave,

Using my magic to help and save,

Granting wishes and doing my best,

To make people smile and bring happiness."

CONTENTS

CHAPTER ONE

A New Adventure

"If you have friends you're never alone.
Seeing a friend is like coming home …"

Mia sang along to the song that was
playing as she stuck glitter on a cardboard
photo frame she was decorating. The song
was from Alice De Silver's latest album.
Alice had been Mia and her best friend
Charlotte's babysitter when they were little,

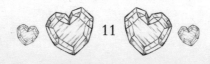

but now she was a famous pop star with hit songs around the world!

Elsie, Mia's four-year-old sister, skipped into the kitchen. She had on a pink tutu over her jeans, a silver wand in her hand and wings on her back. "I'm a fairy ballerina!" she said, spinning around. "Look at me, Mia."

Mia stopped singing. "You look beautiful," she said, smiling.

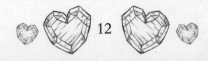

"Don't stop," Elsie cried. "I like your singing. You're so good you should be on *Talent Quest*!"

Talent Quest was Mia's favourite TV programme. She'd loved watching it ever since Alice had been on the show two years ago – and won!

"Sing!" Elsie commanded, tapping Mia with her wand. "Fairy Silverwings wants you to sing!"

"No, Elsie!" Mia said, embarrassed. She loved to sing but only when she was on her own, or with Charlotte. She was too shy to sing in front of other people, even Elsie. "Why don't you dance instead?"

Elsie didn't need any encouraging.

Putting her arms above her head she twirled around the room waving her wand in time to the music, before stopping and curtseying at the end of the song. Mia smiled and clapped. "Your dancing's getting really good, Elsie."

"One day I'll be just as good as Charlotte," Elsie said. She sat down on the kitchen bench beside Mia and sighed. "I miss Charlotte. She always used to teach me new dance steps. I wish she hadn't moved away to America."

"She's going to come back and visit one day," Mia said.

"But I want to see her *now*," Elsie said, her bottom lip sticking out.

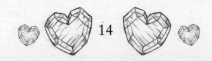

Mia thought fast. How could she cheer up Elsie? "Hey, I've got an idea. Why don't you put another costume on and do a dance to a different Alice song?"

Elsie's face brightened. "OK!" She ran out of the kitchen to get changed.

Mia looked at the photo that she was planning to put in the frame. It was of her and Charlotte after they had been baking one day. They both had flour on their noses, and huge grins, as they held up a plate of cakes with rainbow-coloured sprinkles.

I'm so lucky, Mia thought. Unlike Elsie, she didn't need to be sad about Charlotte moving away because she still got to see her! She and Charlotte shared a wonderful

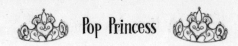

secret – they were training to be Secret
Princesses! Just before Charlotte had moved
away, Alice had given them both matching
magical gold necklaces. Three times now,
the necklaces had whisked Charlotte and
Mia away to meet at an enchanted place
called Wishing Star Palace, where they met
all the Secret Princesses who used magic to
make people's wishes come true!

Mia's fingers went to the necklace around
her neck and she pulled the pendant out
from under her top. It was in the shape of
half a heart and it had three diamonds
embedded in it. She and Charlotte had each
been given a diamond at the end of their
three adventures because they'd granted

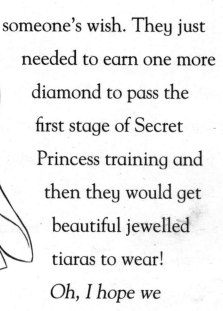

someone's wish. They just needed to earn one more diamond to pass the first stage of Secret Princess training and then they would get beautiful jewelled tiaras to wear!

Oh, I hope we can go to Wishing Star Palace soon, Mia thought excitedly.

The pendant started to sparkle and Mia's heart leapt. The magic was happening again! She glanced around quickly to check she was completely alone. Elsie was still getting changed. Excitement fizzed through

her as the necklace shone.

"I wish I could see Charlotte," Mia whispered quickly.

Bright light blazed out, making the cosy kitchen glow. With a delighted gasp, Mia felt herself being swept up into the light and spinning away. She was off on another magical adventure!

Mia felt her feet touch the ground and opened her eyes. The magic had transported her to the gardens of Wishing Star Palace as it floated high up in the clouds. Bright flowers filled the flowerbeds, while puffs of candyfloss and lollipops hung from the trees' branches. She looked down and saw that her jeans and top had transformed into her beautiful, golden princess dress. The full skirt was covered with delicate embroidery and she had a big bow at her waist and matching ballet shoes. She touched her head and felt the plain gold tiara that had magically appeared in her hair.

"Mia!"

Mia looked around.

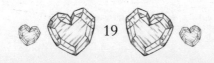

"Up here!"

Charlotte was sitting high up in the branches of a nearby tree. She gave a wide grin as she waved. "I saw some toffee apples in this tree!"

She scrambled down from the tree with two toffee apples in her hand. "Here," she said, handing one to Mia. "They look really yummy!"

"They do," said Mia, hugging her. "Oh, I'm so happy to see you!"

"Me, too!" Charlotte exclaimed. "I wonder whose wish we'll grant this time," she said, biting into her toffee apple and getting flecks of sticky candy stuck to the end of her nose. "And where we'll go."

"I really liked going to Camp Sunshine and helping Laura," said Mia, remembering their last adventure. "Do you remember how homesick and lonely she felt when we first got there?"

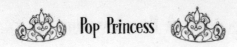

"We helped her make lots of friends," said Charlotte proudly. "Even though Princess Poison tried her best to stop us. Go us!"

Mia gave a shiver. "I hope we don't see Princess Poison again."

Princess Poison had been a Secret Princess, but she had turned bad. Now she wanted to take over Wishing Star Palace. She was very mean and loved using magic to make people unhappy. Every time Princess Poison spoiled a wish, she grew even more powerful and the palace crumbled a bit.

The first time they'd visited, the palace had looked rather shabby. But now, thanks to the wishes Mia and Charlotte had

granted, three of its four turrets had been
repaired. The golden tiles on them sparkled
in the sunlight and the glass in the heart-
shaped windows was no longer cracked.
Only one turret still needed repairing.

"Even if we do see
Princess Poison, we
won't let her stop
us," Charlotte
declared. "We'll
grant someone's
wish, fix the
palace, and
get our fourth
diamonds." She
linked arms with Mia.

"Come on. Let's go inside and see if we can find the Secret Princesses!"

Charlotte and Mia hurried towards the palace, talking and eating their toffee apples as they went. As they got closer, they could hear the sounds of laughter and singing coming from inside.

"It sounds like everyone is having fun!" said Charlotte, taking Mia's hand.

They ran to the palace door and were about to pull it open when they heard a loud noise from inside. *CRASH!*

"Oh, no!" said Mia. "Something's wrong!"

CHAPTER TWO
Spring Cleaning

The girls rushed up to the palace door and Charlotte pulled it open. They both ran into the grand entrance hall and stopped in their tracks, their eyes wide.

All the Secret Princesses were skating around the shining floor with dusters attached to their sparkly slippers, and feather dusters in their hands. As they slid

across the marble floor, they were dusting the walls and pictures.

Two princesses, one with red hair and a dark green dress, and one with a red dress and strawberry-blonde hair, were lying in a heap on the floor, giggling.

"Sorry!" called Princess Sylvie, as she helped the princess in the red dress to her feet. "I spun out of control!"

Mia grinned. That must have been the crash they'd heard!

"It's OK!" giggled the other princess. As she stood up she caught sight of the girls.

"Mia! Charlotte!" she cried.

"Alice!" said Mia happily.

Alice glided over to them and pirouetted

around them gracefully. "You're just in time to help us with the cleaning!"

"Cleaning?" echoed Charlotte in surprise. "I didn't think princesses did cleaning."

"It's fun working together as a team," said Alice. "Look, I'll show you!"

She pulled out her wand and pointed it at the girls. There was a flash and suddenly they both had dusters attached to their shoes and feather dusters in their hands. "This way!" called Alice, skating away across the floor.

Mia and Charlotte pushed one foot in front of the other and found themselves whizzing across the floor. "Wheee!" cried Charlotte. "It's like ice skating!"

Mia glided after her, dusting a window ledge as she twirled. *Alice is right. This really is fun!* she thought.

Charlotte sped around the room, going faster and faster, weaving in and out of the other princesses, who called out greetings as she passed. Then she turned and started skating backwards.

Alice slid over to Mia. "I'm so glad you're here. All the Secret Princesses take part in our annual spring clean, and we didn't want you to miss out on the fun!"

Charlotte jumped, turning in the air and stopping in front of them. Her brown eyes were sparkling. "I wish it was this much fun doing my chores at home!"

"Let's see what's going on in the sitting room," said Alice. "Princess Sophie and Princess Evie are redecorating it."

They skated over to the sitting room. Princess Evie was watering a beautiful display of orchids and Princess Sophie was putting the finishing touches to a large mural of Wishing Star Palace. Princess Sophie was very good at art and had a paintbrush pendant on her necklace. Princess Evie was a talented gardener and had a flower pendant on hers. Each of the princesses had a different shaped pendant, depending on their special talent. Alice's was a musical note because she was so good at singing and Mia and Charlotte's

half-heart pendants meant they had a
special talent for friendship. One day,
if they completed their training, they'd
be a rare kind of Secret Princess called
Friendship Princesses. These always came
in pairs and were very powerful because
they worked together as a team.

Princess Sophie glanced around. "Hi, girls.
Do you like my painting?"

"It's beautiful," said Mia. "It looks just like
the real palace."

"It will look even more like it in a
moment." Princess Sophie pointed her wand
at the picture on the wall and it came to
life! The purple flags on the turrets fluttered,
the birds flew above them and the clouds

floated slowly across the blue sky.

"Oh, wow!" Mia gasped.

One of the cherry trees gave a little shake. Pink blossom fell to the ground, like a shower of pink confetti, while new blossom grew back straight away on the branches.

"There! Now it's much better," said Princess Sophie, with a smile.

Princess Evie held out the gold velvet curtains. "I think these need updating. What do you think? Rose?" She waved her wand and the curtains were suddenly made of pink silk. "Or lilac?" She waved her wand and they changed again to purple satin. "Or how about white with bluebells?" The curtains transformed into floaty white

fabric with pretty blue flowers. "What do you think, girls?" Princess Evie asked Mia and Charlotte. But before they could reply, the flower on the tip of Princess Evie's wand started to glow. Glancing around, Mia saw that the other princesses' wands were shining too.

"Someone's wish needs granting!" she exclaimed.

"This could be our chance to get our final diamond," said Charlotte eagerly.

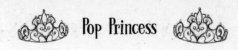

Alice grinned at them. "I guess that means that you're ready do some more wish magic?"

Mia and Charlotte's eyes met. "Oh, yes!" they cried.

The girls hurried after Alice to the Mirror Room, in a turret of the palace. The Magic Mirror swirled with golden and silver light, and a rhyme was already shining in the glass. Charlotte read it out:

"Your magic training is underway
Someone needs your help today.
Each wish you grant, a diamond
you will own,
Four will give you your princess crown!"

Alice touched her wand to the mirror
and the light faded to reveal the image of
a girl with dark skin and cool braided hair.
She was sitting in front of a dressing room
mirror, looking very scared.

"That's who we need to help," said Mia.

A new rhyme appeared:

A wish needs granting, adventures await
Call Sam's name, don't hesitate!

"I wonder what Sam's wish is," Charlotte
thought out loud.

"You'll soon find out!" said Alice.
"If you grant her wish, you'll get your final
diamond and save Wishing Star Palace.

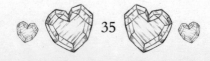

But watch out for Princess Poison and that horrible servant of hers, Hex."

Mia took Charlotte's hand. "We will. Come on, let's hurry."

Charlotte's fingers tightened on Mia's.

"After three. One ... two ... three!"

"Sam!" they both cried.

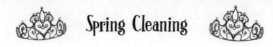

The mirror started to swirl with golden
light and they were sucked into it. They
whooshed down the sparkling tunnel and
shot out at the other end, their feet hitting
solid ground. They blinked and looked
around. Their princess outfits had been
replaced by pretty dresses. Mia's had
a white top with a pink skirt decorated
with red roses. Charlotte's swishy dress was
coral-coloured and sequinned.

Mia glanced down at the cables snaking
across the floor, then up at the big lights
hanging overhead. People dressed in black
scurried all around them. Some of them
spoke into walkie-talkies, others held
clipboards, and two were wheeling a big

piece of scenery along. Nearby, a violinist was practising a tune, dancers in sequinned costumes were stretching their legs, and a short, tubby dog trainer with a long beard was feeding his cross-looking pink poodle some treats.

"Where are we?" Charlotte whispered.

"I have no idea," Mia whispered back. But wherever they were, something exciting was about to happen!

CHAPTER THREE
Talent Quest!

"I think we're backstage in a theatre," whispered Charlotte.

Mia realised she was right. The people in black were stagehands. The others, she guessed, were performers warming up. No one had seemed to notice them arrive, but Mia knew that was all part of the magic, just as no time would pass back home

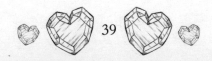

while they were gone. Mia saw a large
sign hanging over the doorway. It said:
Welcome to Talent Quest Ireland!

"Look!" she said, pointing at the sign.
"Do you have *Talent Quest* in America?"
She and Charlotte had both loved the show
back when she lived in the UK.

Charlotte nodded. "America has its own
version of *Talent Quest*," she explained. "So
do lots of other countries."

A man in a grey suit with a funny beard
and a red bow tie came striding through
the backstage area. He was surrounded by a
group of people, all taking notes as he told
them what he wanted them to do.

Mia caught her breath. "It's Richard

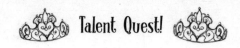

Quincy!" He was the head judge on the UK version of the show – the version Alice had won. Mia guessed he was a judge on the Irish version, too.

The three other judges followed Richard Quincy out onto the stage. "And here are the rest of your judges!" the announcer called. "Sean Casey, Molly Ryan and Antonia Arsenic!"

Three other judges came through the backstage area – a small, cheerful-looking man with red hair who waved and smiled at everyone; a pretty woman with pink curls who blew kisses and called, "Good luck!" to the contestants; and a tall, skinny woman with very high heels on. She had a

sharp blonde bob and she was wearing huge
sunglasses even though they were indoors.
Mia wondered where she had seen her
before. Maybe she'd been on the UK *Talent
Quest* as well.

"Next up, we have teenage ballroom
dancing stars, Leon and Leona!" the
announcer said.

A girl and boy waltzed onto the stage.

Mia wished she could stay and watch but
they had a job to do.

"Sam must be here somewhere," she said.
"Let's find her."

Just then a man with a walkie-talkie
hurried up to them. "Hi, girls. Which act
are you with?"

"Um, Sam," said Charlotte.

"She's in dressing room nine," he said, pointing to a sign saying 'Dressing Rooms'. "Tell her it's almost her turn on stage."

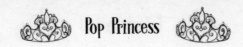

Following the sign, Charlotte and Mia
went down a staircase and through a
door. It led into a waiting room with lots
of sofas. There were more people in there,
rehearsing, chatting and drinking coffee.
All around there was a flurry of activity.

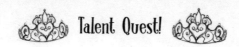

Make-up artists were applying powder
with large brushes, costume people were
adjusting outfits and hairdressers were
brushing hair into glamorous styles.

"This is so exciting!" breathed Charlotte,
gazing around with wide eyes.

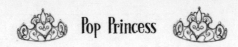

Charlotte loved to dance and Mia knew her friend had always dreamed of being on TV. But Mia felt out of place here. She'd much rather watch television than be a TV star herself!

Mia looked up at a large TV screen on the wall that was showing what was happening on stage.

The judges were talking to Leon and Leona, who had just finished dancing.

"You were really good, guys," Molly Ryan said, twirling one of her pink curls around her finger and smiling encouragingly at the ballroom dancers. "But you need a little more practice."

"You must keep going," said Sean Casey.

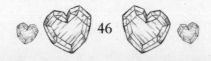

"Don't be put off by one little tumble. You have real talent, my dears."

"Well, I think it was ghastly, simply ghastly!" Antonia Arsenic, the blonde-haired lady, drawled from behind her sunglasses.

"Wow, she's mean!" Mia said, as the dancers both looked upset.

"She is," said Charlotte. "But we'd better not stay and watch this any longer. We've got to find Sam."

Mia followed Charlotte down the corridor to a door marked with the number nine. Charlotte knocked.

"Come in," a girl's voice said.

They opened the door and saw the girl

from the Magic Mirror. Sam was sitting in a chair with her guitar on her knees. Her hair was tied back in long, delicate braids and her face was damp with tears. "Hi, can I help you?" she said, quickly wiping her eyes. Mia didn't know what to say, but Charlotte was already speaking confidently. "Hi, we've been sent to tell you that they need you by the stage soon."

"OK, thanks." Sam gave them a weak smile. "Are you contestants too?"

"No, we're just helping here today," said Charlotte. "I'm Charlotte and this is Mia."

"I'm Samira," the girl said, with a sniff. "But everyone calls me Sam."

"Are you OK?" Mia said to Sam.

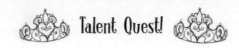

Sam swallowed and looked down at her guitar. Mia went over to her. "What's wrong?" she said gently.

"I just wish I could win," Sam said. "It would change my family's lives if I became a pop star. I want to make them proud of me."

"I'm sure they *are* proud of you," said Mia. "I bet they'll be cheering louder than anyone else in the audience."

Sam's eyes filled with tears again. "That's the thing. They were supposed to be here but they phoned me to say they're stuck in traffic. Now I won't have anyone supporting me out there. I'm feeling so nervous that I'm sure I'll forget my song!"

Mia glanced at Charlotte, wondering what they could do. Their necklaces would let them grant three wishes. However, they couldn't just wish for Sam to win the contest. Their wish magic wasn't powerful enough for that; besides, it wouldn't be fair to the other contestants. But maybe they

could help Sam feel less lonely so she could go out there and sing her very best? They might not even need magic for that.

"Why don't you practise your song by singing it for us?" Mia suggested.

"That's a great idea," said Charlotte. "We'd love to hear you sing, and it would be a good warm-up for you."

"Well, OK," said Sam shyly. She picked up her guitar. "My song's called 'We're Strong When We're Together'."

She strummed a couple of chords and began to sing in a sweet voice:

"*You are my rock, you are my everything,*
When I'm with you, it makes me want
to sing …"

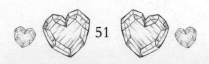

Mia and Charlotte moved closer together, listening to Sam's beautiful voice. Her song ended with the final line:

"*Together with you, I can do anything.*"

Sam lowered her guitar and looked hopefully at them. "Well? Was that OK?"

"It was more than OK," Mia exclaimed, clapping hard. "It was amazing!"

"It's a great song," said Charlotte.

Sam smiled. "Thanks. I wrote it for my family. They make me feel like I can follow my dreams and achieve anything I want. I don't know what I'd do without them."

"I know that feeling," said Mia. "Being with my best friend makes me feel exactly like that."

Charlotte smiled at her. "Me, too."

"I bet the judges will love it," Mia told Sam. "And they'll love you. You really don't need to be nervous. Even if your family don't make it in time, you'll be fine."

Sam took a deep breath. "You're both sure it was OK?"

"Oh, yes!" the girls chorused.

Just then, there was a knock on the door. A stagehand poked his head around the door and said, "Come to the stage now, Sam. It's show time!"

CHAPTER FOUR
Make a Wish

"Will you come with me?" Sam asked the girls nervously.

"Of course," Mia said. "We'll stand in the wings and listen to you sing. That way, even if your family isn't here, you'll have us supporting you."

"Thank you," Sam said, with a smile. "That will really help."

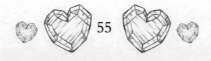

They left her dressing room and hurried up the stairs to the wings. Thick red curtains kept the waiting contestants hidden from the stage, but you could just about see what was happening on the stage.

The small fat man with a long beard was trying to persuade his pink poodle to bark a song. He was wearing a top hat and a suit with long coat tails and a pink bow tie that matched the poodle. The dog was standing on a box and woofing randomly to the music. The audience started to boo. The poodle gave up and turned its back grumpily on the man.

"Sing, Miss Fluffy!" the tubby man commanded. "Sing, I tell you!" He tried to

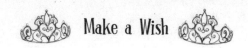

conduct it with his hands. "Sing!"

The poodle looked away snootily.
The audience started to laugh. "Off! Off!
Off!" they chanted.

Charlotte grinned. "I think it's time to
press the *paws* button and say *poodle-oo*!"

Mia groaned. "Charlotte! Your jokes get worse all the time!"

"You love them, though," said Charlotte, nudging her.

The little man swung round in a huff and marched off the stage. The poodle jumped down and followed him, its nose in the air.

Sam grinned. "At least I won't be the worst act out there."

As the little man came off stage, Mia couldn't resist stooping down to say hello to the poodle. She loved all animals – even grumpy dogs!

"Hi, there," she murmured, holding out her hand for it to sniff.

"Grrr!" the poodle snapped at her crossly.

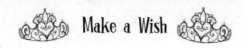

Mia quickly jumped back in surprise.

"Go on, Miss Fluffy!" hissed the man, his face hidden by his bushy beard and top hat. "Now's your chance!"

The poodle darted past Mia and bit the strings on Sam's guitar. It pulled back hard. The strings stretched.

"Get off!" gasped Sam, trying to pull the guitar away.

"Make your dog stop!" Charlotte cried to the little man. But he didn't do anything.

"Grrrr-rrrrrr!" snarled the poodle, shaking its head. With a horrible *twang* the strings snapped. The guitar was broken!

"Oh, no!" wailed Sam.

The man sniggered. "Whoopsie!"

Mia and Charlotte gasped. Charlotte leapt forwards and pushed the man's top hat back.

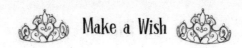

"Hex!" she cried. It was Princess Poison's horrible servant, disguised by a fake beard. "What are you doing here?"

"Stopping her wish from coming true, of course," he hissed, pointing at Sam, who was crying as she examined her broken guitar. "And it looks like we've succeeded! She won't be able to sing without a guitar, so she won't win the contest." He gave a mean giggle. "Come on, Miss Fluffy. You're a very good dog!"

The poodle yapped happily. She and Hex pushed past the girls and disappeared into the crowd.

Mia ran to Sam. "Oh, no! Look at your poor guitar."

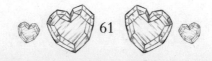

"It's ruined," said Sam, tears streaking down her face. "And I can't afford to buy another. My mum saved up for ages to buy this one."

"Don't worry, we can fix it," said Charlotte. She held up her pendant and showed it to Mia. It was glowing with light. Mia pulled her own necklace out from the top of her dress. Hers was glowing too. Excitement raced through her. She knew exactly what Charlotte was thinking.

It was time to use some wish magic!

"Come over here, Sam," said Charlotte, guiding Sam behind a piece of scenery where no one would see them. She held her necklace out towards Mia. Mia brought her own pendant to meet it. The two halves of the heart fit together perfectly.

"I wish Sam had a new guitar, one that's perfect for her," said Mia.

There was a flash of golden light and Sam gasped. Her old guitar vanished and in its place was a brand-new guitar. It was white with glittering silver and gold stars all over it. "Oh, my goodness!" she stammered. "This is the guitar I've always wanted.

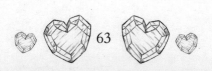

I used to see it in the shop where I buy my guitar music. What … how …?"

"It's magic," Mia said. Sam looked amazed. "I know it sounds crazy, but it really *is* magic."

"Mia and I can grant wishes," Charlotte went on. "We're training to become Secret Princesses – kind of like fairy godmothers."

Sam blinked.

"It's true," Mia told her. "We were sent here to help you today, but you mustn't tell anyone. Our magic's got to stay secret."

Charlotte nodded. "We can grant you three wishes. The guitar was the first one."

"I can't believe it," said Sam, looking down at the guitar and then back at them.

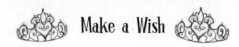

"But I guess it's got to be true."

"It is," Mia told her. "And we'll do all we can to help you. But we can't use a wish to make you win the competition. You have to win it with your own talent."

"But you can do it," Charlotte said, as Sam stepped out from behind the piece of scenery, still looking dazed. "We both believe in you. We really do."

"Ah, there you are, Sam." The stage manager with a clipboard hurried up to her. "The judges are just taking a quick break and then you're on. Oh, dear," she said in concern. "Your make-up seems to have smudged." Sam's tears had left mascara streaking down her face.

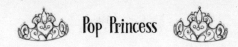
"There's just time for you to nip down and see one of the make-up artists. They'll soon sort you out."

As she spoke, Antonia Arsenic, the judge with the blonde bob, came clacking across the floor in her green high heels. "There's no need for that. I can do it," she said breezily, wrapping her hand around

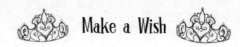

Sam's arm. "I'm *very* good with make-up."
Antonia gave Sam a smile, flashing dazzling
white teeth. "Come with me, my sweet."

Sam went off with her.

"Mia," Charlotte said slowly, staring
after the judge. "Does she remind you of
someone?"

"Yes, but I can't think who," said Mia.

"Imagine her in a green dress. If she
had long dark hair with an ice-blonde
streak ..." Charlotte said.

Mia's eyes widened. "Princess Poison!"

As the girls stared after them, the judge
looked back over her shoulder – and with
a flash of green, her hair changed. It *was*
Princess Poison!

"She must be trying to stop us granting Sam's wish!" Charlotte gasped.

"We should have realised from her name – arsenic is a type of poison!" Mia cried in dismay, as icy fingers ran down her spine. "Oh, no, we have to find where Princess Poison is taking Sam!"

CHAPTER FIVE
Princess Poison Strikes Again

Charlotte and Mia raced after Princess Poison and Sam, but they'd already disappeared backstage. The girls charged down the stairs and back into the waiting room, almost knocking over a juggler, but they couldn't see Princess Poison or Sam anywhere.

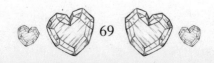

"The show's about to start again!" one of the contestants who was watching the TV monitor called.

Charlotte grabbed Mia's hand. "We'd better go back to the stage and see if Sam is there."

Mia nodded. Her heart was pounding. What was Princess Poison going to do?

They ran back up the stairs, taking them two at a time. Reaching the top they saw Sam standing in the wings at the side of the stage. She had her back to them. "Sam!" Mia gasped in relief. Then Sam turned and Mia's hands flew to her mouth.

Sam's make-up was awful! She had big black circles around her eyes, two bright red spots of blusher on her cheeks and sickly yellow lipstick. Her hair had been partly unbraided and combed into a messy bird's nest of curls. She looked dreadful!

"Hi," she smiled, seeing them. "I was wondering where you went. Antonia Arsenic is actually really lovely. She took me to her private dressing room and did my hair and make-up herself. She wouldn't let me look in the mirror, though – she said it was bad luck. What do you think?"

Mia opened and shut her mouth, not knowing what to say. Even Charlotte was at a loss for words.

"I look OK, don't I?" Sam said anxiously, seeing their faces.

"Um … well … you…" Mia's voice came out as a strangled squeak.

"What is it?" said Sam. Seeing a mirror at the side of the stage, she went over to look in it. When she saw her reflection, she shrieked in horror.

"Sssh!" hushed one of the stage crew.

"My hair! My face!" Sam turned to the girls in dismay.

"I can't go on stage like this!"

"No, you really can't," said Charlotte. She grabbed her pendant. It was still glowing, but more faintly now. "Luckily we still have two wishes left."

"Sam, come to the stage now, please!" called the stage manager.

Mia pulled out her pendant. They had to make another wish straight away – there wasn't a single second to waste! The girls pushed their necklaces together. "I wish Sam looked amazing!" said Charlotte.

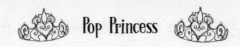

FLASH!

There was a burst of golden light and Sam was magically transformed! Her hair suddenly fell in perfect ringlets and her make-up was lovely – a hint of pink on her lips and shimmery eye-shadow that made her eyes look even browner. Her clothes had changed too. Her top and jeans had

turned into a silver and white jumpsuit that matched her new guitar.

"You look incredible!" Mia told her.

"I love it!" Sam gasped. "This outfit's awesome. Thank you!"

She ran to the side of the stage where the stage manager was waiting for her. Mia and Charlotte followed her.

Finlay O'Hara, the show's presenter, motioned to the wings. "Now we have our final contestant, the lovely Samira James. Please give our youngest contestant a big hand and welcome Sam to the stage!"

"On you go," the stage manager said, nodding at her.

"Good luck!" called Mia and Charlotte.

Sam walked onstage with her guitar.

There were several television monitors at the side of the stage. One showed the stage from the front, another showed the audience and the judges. Mia and Charlotte could see the four judges sitting at their table. The other judges were clapping, but Princess Poison was sitting with her arms crossed. Her blonde wig was gone, but her magic meant that no one else had noticed.

She scowled as she saw Sam's new look.

"Do you think we should make another wish to help Sam?" Mia asked Charlotte. Their necklaces were still glowing, but only very faintly – they just had one wish left.

"We could wish that she gets a standing ovation – that would impress the judges," Charlotte suggested.

"She'll get that on her own," said Mia. On the monitor, she watched Sam scan the audience. Her face fell as she looked at the area where the contestants' families sat. There were still empty seats. It looked as though Sam's family hadn't made it.

An idea popped into Mia's mind. "Let's wish that her family was here! Seeing them

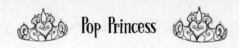

will make her really happy and hopefully help her sing her best."

Charlotte smiled. "Brilliant plan!" They touched their pendants together. "We wish that Sam's family could be here," said Charlotte. Light flickered across the pendants and then faded. Mia bit her lip nervously.

"Do you think it's worked?" said Charlotte.

To Mia's relief, she saw a huge grin spread across Sam's face as she waved out at the audience.

The audience monitor showed a group of people making their way through the auditorium to the family seating area.

"Samira's family have managed to join us!" said Finlay. "You were cutting it fine," he said, giving them a cheeky grin. "But you've made it just in time to hear your girl perform and that's all that matters. Over to you, Sam!"

Sam beamed and strummed the first chord on her new guitar. The band joined in. She began to sing:

"You are my rock, you are my everything,
When I'm with you, I want to sing …"

Sam sounded even more amazing on stage with the microphone, the band and the backing singers joining in.

"She's got to win!" whispered Charlotte. "She's brilliant!"

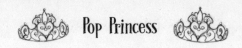

In the monitor, they could see three of
the judges smiling, but Princess Poison was
scowling. Mia saw her hand move slightly.
"Charlotte – look!" she gasped, pointing to
the wand just visible in Princess Poison's
hand. "She's going to put a spell on Sam!"

"Oh, no, she's not," said Charlotte.
Looking around wildly, she grabbed a
juggling ball that someone had left behind.

Then she ran to the side of the stage and pushed the curtain aside.

Through the gap, Mia could see Princess Poison pointing her wand at Sam and moving her lips.

Charlotte took aim and threw the juggling ball. *Whack!* It knocked the wand out of Princess Poison's hand, just as

horrid green magic began to shoot out of it.

Princess Poison let out a howl of anger.

"Great shot, Charlotte!" Mia exclaimed.

Charlotte grinned. "I'm on the softball team at my new school."

But her smile faded when one of the backing singers grabbed her tummy. Then another did the same, and then another. They all started to run off the stage,

clutching their stomachs.

"Wait! What's the matter?" said Sam, stopping mid-song.

"Oh, dear," Charlotte whispered to Mia. "The bad magic missed Sam, but some of it must have hit the backing singers."

Sam followed the backing singers offstage, calling, "Are you OK?"

The audience broke into uproar and the band stopped playing.

"Sam! Sam! Come back!" called Finlay, looking horrified.

Richard Quincy stood up. "Get her back out here. If she doesn't finish her song, she'll be eliminated from the competition."

"Oh, dear," Princess Poison said, smirking

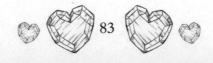

straight into the camera. "Those backing singers don't look very well. It must be something they ate backstage. What a pity. I guess Samira's dreams are over."

Charlotte and Mia ran over to Sam, who was standing backstage looking dismayed.

"Go back on," Charlotte urged her. "You have to finish your song or you'll lose your place in the competition."

"But I can't sing in front of everyone without the backing singers," said Sam.

"You can! You've just got to be brave," said Mia.

"Sam, you really need to go back on!" the stage manager said urgently.

"How about we sing with you?" said Charlotte suddenly. "We can be your backing singers, can't we, Mia?"

"We can?" Mia squeaked, her tummy dropping at the thought of going on stage and singing in front of all the people out there – and everyone watching on TV.

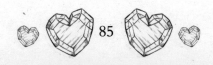

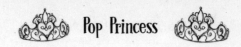

"Yes!" Charlotte grabbed her hand. "We have to do this. Sam needs us!"

Mia felt butterflies starting to flap inside her. But she knew she couldn't tell Sam to be brave and then refuse to be brave herself.

"Please sing with me," Sam said desperately.

Mia caught Charlotte's eye and took a deep breath. "Of course we will," she said.

CHAPTER SIX
And the Winner Is ...

Sam gave Mia and Charlotte a huge hug. "Thank you!" She turned and ran back on to the stage. The audience was clapping and chanting her name.

Charlotte grabbed Mia's hand. "We'd better get out there!"

Mia let Charlotte pull her onto the stage towards the backing singers' microphones.

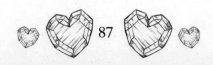

The stage lights were so bright it made it very hard to see beyond the first couple of rows of seats. Somehow that made her feel less afraid. If she couldn't see the audience looking at her, she could almost imagine they weren't there.

"You!" Princess Poison pointed at Sam. "What are *you* doing back on stage? You haven't got any backing singers to sing with."

"Oh, yes, she has," Charlotte said loudly, stepping forwards. "She's got us!"

A look of fury crossed Princess Poison's face. "Those two girls shouldn't be on stage!" she snapped to the other judges. "Get them off!"

"No," Richard Quincy interrupted. "The show must go on. As long as they're happy to sing, that's all that matters."

He smiled at Sam. "When you're ready, you can start your song again from the beginning, Samira."

Mia's tummy felt like it was tying itself in knots. Charlotte seemed to sense her nerves and squeezed her hand. "You'll be fine," she whispered. "Just pretend we're singing along to one of Alice's songs together."

Mia squeezed Charlotte's hand back.

Sam glanced across at them and started to sing. As she reached the chorus they joined in with her.

"*You are my rock, you are my everything*
When I'm with you, I want to sing …"

Mia sang with Charlotte, their voices rising in perfect harmony with Sam's.

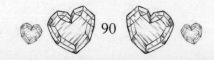

They smiled at each other as they sang and Mia felt all her panic and fear fade away. She was singing an amazing song on television with her best friend. How incredible was that?

They reached the end of the song and the whole audience erupted into cheers. All the judges apart from Princess Poison stood up, clapping.

"That was wonderful, simply wonderful," said Molly Ryan, wiping away a tear. "So much emotion."

"Oh, Samira, you little treasure! You have so much talent," said Sean Casey.

Richard Quincy smiled. "Well done, Sam. That was truly electrifying."

"Well, I disagree!" said Princess Poison.
"Bah!" she snapped. "Who wants to listen
to some silly girl whining about her family
giving her strength? Give *me* strength if
I have to listen to that twaddle! The poodle
should win! It's got more talent in one little
claw than *she*'s got in her whole body!"

The audience went quiet.
Mia saw Sam's eyes fill
with tears.

"Blah, blah, blah,
oh, I love my family
and my friends,"
Princess Poison
mocked cruelly.
"Blah, blah, blah, blah,

they mean so much to me." Her eyes grew icy. "Well, my dear, do us all a favour – get off the stage and go back to them." She gave a shrill laugh.

Anger rushed through Mia. *How dare Princess Poison be so mean!* "You don't know what you're talking about!" she exclaimed, running forwards. "Sam's song isn't rubbish. It's brilliant. Your family and friends *do* give you strength."

Charlotte joined her. "Mia's right. Having family and friends is the most important thing in the whole world. Sam deserves to win! She's really talented, and her song is brilliant!"

The audience started cheering.

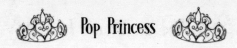

Richard Quincy smiled. "Looks like you've got a couple of really good friends there," he said to Sam. "Thank you, girls. Well, let's bring everyone else back on and vote."

Finlay brought the other contestants back onto the stage – the teenage ballroom dancers, a ballerina, a magician, a fire-eater, a violinist, the juggler and Hex with his pink poodle. The dog looked just as grumpy as before and growled at the ballerina standing next to Hex. Mia and Charlotte stood next to Sam, each holding one of her hands.

"So," Finlay said to the judges. "Have you made your decision? Remember – you must all agree or the decision will be handed over to our studio audience."

Richard Quincy smiled at Sam and the girls. "I agree with everything Samira's backing singers said. Sam gets my vote."

The audience cheered wildly.

"Mine, too," said Sean Casey.

Molly Ryan looked at the other contestants. "You all did very well," she said kindly. "But Samira gets my vote today."

"Well, she doesn't get mine!" snapped Princess Poison. She pointed at Hex and the pink poodle. "I want the poodle to win!"

The audience started to boo loudly.

Finlay held up his hand for quiet. "In that case, the audience decides. Fingers on your voting buttons, please. The contestant who

gets the most audience votes in the next ten seconds will be declared the winner." There was a drumroll. "You have ten seconds to decide the winner," Finlay cried. "Press your voting buttons NOW!"

The clock started to count down. The audience pressed their buttons. Princess Poison jumped to her feet – and in her hand was her wand.

Charlotte and Mia both gasped in horror. "She's going to use magic again, and we don't have any wishes left!" Mia whispered in dismay.

"Woof!"

The poodle leapt out of Hex's grip and raced across the stage. Jumping up onto the

judges' table, it bit the wand.

"It thinks it's a stick!" Charlotte hissed to Mia, as Princess Poison shrieked and tried to pull the wand away.

"Three, two, one ..." Finlay counted down. There was a blare of horns.

"And the winner is ..." Finlay said.

Sam's photo appeared on the screen!

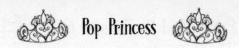

"Samira James!" he bellowed.

The audience exploded into cheers and shouts. Mia and Charlotte jumped up and down with excitement. Princess Poison finally wrestled the wand away from the poodle and stamped her foot in fury.

"Thank you! Thank you!" Sam told the girls. "I never would have won without you!" She hugged them both tightly. "I do believe in magic now. I really do!" Confetti showered down from above.

"It's a fix!" cried Princess Poison, storming onto the stage. "I demand a recount! She can't be the winner! She—"

The poodle jumped at the wand again. It missed, but its teeth caught the hem of

Princess Poison's skirt. The poodle pulled
backwards, tugging at the material. There
was a tearing sound and her skirt started
to rip. The poodle tugged even harder.
Princess Poison shrieked and ran
off the stage, clutching the
remains of her skirt. Hex
tried to pull the poodle off.

"Stop it, Miss Fluffy! Stop it!"

The poodle turned and bit his ankle.

"Ow!" he yelled.

"Oh, dear, that poodle's really in the dog house now!" Charlotte said, with a giggle.

Sam hugged Mia and Charlotte again. "This is the best day of my life. My wish really has come true!"

Golden flashes of light exploded around them. The audience gasped, assuming it was special effects, but Mia knew it was magic. "We did it!" she said, grabbing Charlotte's hand happily.

"We really did!" Charlotte said. "We granted Sam's wish! And now we'll get our fourth diamond!"

"And we stopped Princess Poison, so Wishing Star Palace will be fixed!" added Mia excitedly.

The two girls squeezed each others' hands tightly and squealed with joy.

"I don't think today could get any better," Charlotte said, sighing happily. But she was wrong ...

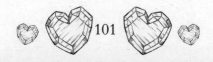

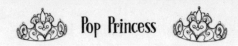

"Now it's time to invite someone very special to present the prize!" said Finlay. "Please welcome *Talent Quest* winner and international singing sensation, Alice De Silver, to the stage!"

CHAPTER SEVEN
Celebration!

Mia and Charlotte swung around as Alice came on stage in a gorgeous sparkly silver dress. "Sam truly deserves to win!" she told the audience. "I love her song. In fact, I love it so much I'd like to sing it with her. Would that be OK, Sam?"

"Yes!" breathed Sam, looking star-struck.

"Can my friends join in too?"

Alice looked over at Mia and Charlotte and winked. "Definitely!"

The music started and they all began to sing. Mia didn't even feel nervous, because she was just so happy for Sam.

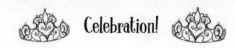

When they reached the very last
line – "*Together with you I can do
anything*"– Sam's family came running
onto the stage, hugging her.

"You've made Sam's wish come true,"
Alice murmured to Mia and Charlotte.
"I'm so proud of you both. You encouraged
her and gave her confidence, and even sang
with her in front of thousands of people."
She gave Mia a special smile. "You've been
so brave and such good friends to her. Come
with me."

She beckoned them into the wings. They
followed her behind one of the curtains and
she pulled out her wand and touched it to
their necklaces. There was a flash of light

and another diamond appeared in their pendants. "Your fourth diamond!" she said, beaming. "Quick, hold hands!"

They took one last peek around the curtain at Sam smiling happily with all her family and friends, and then took hold of Alice's hands.

"Hold tight!" she cried. "It's time to go!"

"But where are we going?" gasped Mia.

Usually they went home after granting a wish.

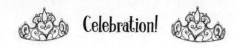

But Alice didn't reply. Her sparkly shoes shone with magic and they spun away, as if they were on a roundabout. Faster and faster they went, spiralling up into the air.

Suddenly, their feet touched soft grass and they heard the sound of birds singing. Opening their eyes, they saw they were in the garden of Wishing Star Palace. They were wearing their princess dresses and plain gold tiaras again.

"The turrets are all mended!" gasped Charlotte. All four turrets were glittering in the sunlight, their tiles all perfectly restored, the glass panes in the heart-shaped windows were sparkling and without a single crack.

"It's fixed, all thanks to you," said Alice.

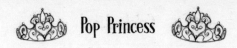

"Let's go inside. The other princesses are waiting to congratulate you."

They followed her up to the door. As she pushed it open, the girls saw all the other Secret Princesses gathered in the entrance hall. They clapped loudly as Charlotte and Mia came in. Princess Evie and Princess Sylvie ran forward to give them a hug.

"Well done, girls!" cried Princess Sylvie. "You stopped Princess Poison again!"

"And you made Sam's wish come true," said Princess Anna, the oldest Secret Princess, whose grey hair was tied back in an elegant bun. "Not just with magic but by being brave and clever, and, most of all, by knowing what friendship really means."

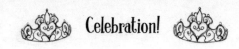

The other princesses crowded round, hugging them and congratulating them.

Mia's head spun. They'd made everyone so happy and proud. It was the best feeling in the world!

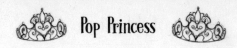

"And now, I think it's time for you to get your true Secret Princess tiaras," said Princess Anna. "Are you ready?"

"Oh, yes!" exclaimed Charlotte. Mia nodded in excitement.

"Then touch your necklaces together," said Princess Anna. Mia and Charlotte did as she said. As the two half-heart pendants fitted together to make a whole heart, golden light surrounded the girls like a sparkling whirlwind.

As the light faded, Mia gasped. "Charlotte! Your tiara!" Her friend's tiara was now studded with beautiful diamonds!

Mia's hand flew to her head. Her own tiara had transformed too!

"You have both passed the first stage of your Secret Princess training,"

announced Princess Anna happily. "You are now one step closer to becoming full Secret Princesses."

Charlotte picked up her half-heart pendant. "The diamonds have disappeared from our necklaces!" she said. There were now just four empty spaces where the gems had been.

"For the next stage of your training you'll
need to grant four more wishes to earn four
rubies. When you have them,
you'll get your Secret
Princess shoes that
will let you travel
magically," said
Princess Anna.

"So we'll get
to have more
adventures?"
Charlotte said
staring at her new
jewelled tiara in excitement.

"And help more people?" asked Mia.

"Yes, and I'm sure you'll have to face

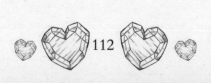

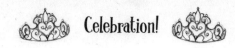

Princess Poison again too," said Alice, stepping forward. "She'll be even more determined to stop you now."

"Just let her try!" said Charlotte.

Mia nodded and linked arms with her. "She won't stop us. It's like Sam's song — together we're stronger. We really can do anything when we're together!"

Alice's eyes met Mia and Charlotte's. "I always thought you'd be perfect Secret Princesses," she said softly. "And with every adventure you prove it more and more." She hugged them, her eyes shining. "It's time for you both to go home now. But you'll see each other again soon."

"I hope it's *very* soon!" said Charlotte.

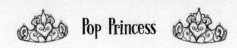

She squeezed Mia's hand. "Bye for now."

"But only for now," said Mia.

Alice waved her wand. Calling goodbye to everyone, Mia and Charlotte were swept away in two separate whirlwinds of light.

Mia landed in her kitchen. It was so weird to be back at home after all the excitement. The kitchen door flew open and Mia jumped as Elsie came running in. She was dressed in a pink princess dress with a plastic tiara on her head.

"Look at me. I'm a princess now!" Elsie cried, twirling around. "Can we dance and play princesses, Mia? Pleeeeease!"

Mia grinned at her. "Of course we can. I'll always play princesses with you."

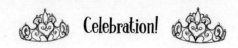

She took Elsie's hands and swung her around, happiness bubbling inside her.

As Mia spun round, Elsie giggled. "Being a princess is fun!" she squealed.

"Yes, it is," Mia agreed, wishing she could tell Elsie that she was training to be one for real. But maybe Elsie would find out about Secret Princesses for herself one day. "It's the best thing in the whole world!"

The End

Join Charlotte and Mia in their next *Secret Princesses* adventure – two magical stories in one!

Read on for a sneak peek!

Snowflake Sisters

"Jingle bells, jingle bells ..."

Mia sang as she sat on her bed, knitting a scarf. Happiness was fizzing through her. It was Christmas – her favourite time of year. She had decorated her bedroom with paper chains and had hung an orange studded with cloves from her wardrobe door. It was making her room smell sweet and spicy.

The scarf was going to be her mum's Christmas present. She couldn't wait to see her mum's face when she unwrapped it on Christmas Day.

Just then, her bedroom door opened. She quickly pushed the scarf under her pillow. But it wasn't her mum, it was her little sister, Elsie.

"Mia! Mia! Look what I made at playgroup!" Elsie said, skipping in, her blonde pigtails bouncing. "But promise you won't tell Mummy. It's a surprise."

"I promise I won't tell," Mia told her sister. "What is it?"

Elsie opened her hands and showed Mia a necklace she had made from pasta shells painted gold. "Do you like it?"

"It's great," Mia said enthusiastically.

"What are you giving Mummy?" Elsie asked her.

Mia pulled the scarf out from under her pillow. "This."

"That's pretty," said Elsie, stroking it. "Are you making a scarf for Charlotte, too?"

Charlotte was Mia's best friend. She used to live nearby, but she and her family had moved to America earlier in the year. "No," said Mia. "It's really hot in California – too hot for scarves."

"Hot? At Christmas time?" said Elsie.

Mia nodded, thinking about the last time she had talked Charlotte on the computer. Charlotte had been wearing shorts!

"So, what are you giving her?" asked Elsie.

"I'm knitting her a Christmas stocking," said Mia. "I'm going to put her favourite

English sweets inside." She had an idea. "Why don't you make her a card? We could post it with my present. She'd love that."

"OK," said Elsie eagerly. "I'll go and get my crayons." She ran off.

Mia thought wistfully about her best friend. They'd always done so much together at Christmas time. They'd gone shopping and carol singing, visited Santa at the local garden centre, made Christmas decorations and baked mince pies together. And, of course, when they were younger, they'd been in the school Nativity play together every year. It was so strange not having her around at Christmas time.

Mia glanced down at the pendant shaped

like half a heart that hung from a golden chain around her neck. Charlotte had the other half of the heart. But they weren't just necklaces, they were part of an amazing secret the girls shared!

Mia could still hardly believe it, but their necklaces were magic! They transported her and Charlotte to a beautiful place called Wishing Star Palace. On their first visit, they had discovered that they'd been chosen to train as Secret Princesses – special people who could use magic to make wishes come true. It was the most amazing thing that had ever happened to her! Best of all, she and Charlotte could see each other every time they met there!

Mia smiled and touched her necklace as she remembered the four Secret Princess adventures she and Charlotte had shared. *We're so lucky,* she thought. It was the best feeling ever when she and Charlotte used magic to make someone happy!

A tingle ran across her fingertips and the pendant started to shine softly. Mia caught her breath as excitement rushed through her.

"I wish I could see Charlotte!" she whispered quickly.

WHOOSH!

Golden light flooded out of the pendant, swirling around her in a sparkling cloud. Mia felt herself being lifted up and carried away in a tunnel of light. For a moment, she wondered what Elsie would say when she came back into her bedroom to find her gone, but then she remembered that time always stood still while she and Charlotte were away on a magical adventure.

Mia's feet touched the ground and she opened her eyes. She was in the garden of Wishing Star Palace, but she'd never seen it look this beautiful. The lawn was covered in a blanket of sparkling snow!

Read *Snowflake Sisters* to find out what happens next!

Friendship Princesses

Friendship Princesses are the rarest type of
Secret Princess because they always come in pairs.
They both need to have all the Secret Princess
qualities, like kindness and bravery, but they
also need a friendship strong enough to withstand
any test. Could you and your best friend be
Friendship Princesses?

When your best friend tells you a secret, you ...

A. Don't tell anyone because your friend trusted you.

B. Feel tempted to tell someone else.

C. Tell the secret to everyone you know.

When you are on holiday, you ...

A. Miss your best friend lots and bring them back a special souvenir.

B. Send them a postcard.

C. Barely think of them – you're having too way much fun!

What would you do if your best friend got something you really wanted?

A. Feel genuinely happy and give them a big hug.

B. Feel a bit jealous, but congratulate them.

C. Say something mean to make them feel bad too.

It's your best friend's birthday. You ...

A. Make them something really special.

B. Let your mum pick out a nice gift.

C. Don't bother getting them a present.

You and your friend have had an argument.
What do you do?

A. Make up as quickly as possible.

B. Wait until they apologise first, then be friends again.

C. Never apologise because you are always right.

Scores

For every **A** answer, give yourself two points.

For every **B** answer, give yourself one point.

For every **C** answer, give yourself zero points.

4-6
You are a good friend, but remember – Friendship Princesses always need to be there for each other.

7-10
Well done! You and your friend have potential to be Friendship Princesses. Keep up the good work!

0-3
Oh, dear. You and your friend are more like Princess Poison and Hex than Mia and Charlotte!

♥ FREE NECKLACE ♥

Secret PRINCESSES

In every book of Secret Princesses series one: The Diamond Collection, there is a special Wish Token. Collect all four tokens to get an exclusive Best Friends necklace by

MONSOON

CHILDREN

for you and your best friend!

Simply fill in the form below, send it in with your four tokens and we'll send you your special necklaces.*

Send to: Secret Princesses Wish Token Offer, Hachette Children's Books Marketing Department, Carmelite House, 50 Victoria Embankment, London, EC4Y 0DZ

Closing Date: 31st December 2016

secretprincessesbooks.co.uk

✂

ase complete using capital letters (UK and Republic of Ireland dents only)

ST NAME:

RNAME:

TE OF BIRTH: DD MM YYYY

DRESS LINE 1:

DRESS LINE 2:

DRESS LINE 3:

STCODE:

RENT OR GUARDIAN'S EMAIL ADDRESS:

I'd like to receive regular Secret Princesses email newsletters and information about other great Hachette Children's Group offers (I can unsubscribe at any time).

I'd like to receive regular Monsoon Children email newsletters (I can unsubscribe at any time).

Terms and Conditions apply. For full terms and conditions please go to secretprincessesbooks.co.uk/terms

1 Secret Princesses Wish Token

* 2000 necklaces available while stocks last. Terms and conditions apply.

Secret
PRINCESSES

What would you wish for?

Are you a Secret Princess?

Join the Secret Princesses Club at:

secretprincessesbooks.co.uk

Explore the magic of the
Secret Princesses and discover:

💗 Special competitions! 💗
💗 Exclusive content! 💗
💗 All the latest princess news! 💗